# Gibbe

by

# Bram Stoker

Golden Flower Publishing

Book Cover by Kathryn McGovern

## Disclaimer

As a work of classic literature, this book might contain language referring to people or places that some may find offensive. While the views expressed do not reflect those of the publisher, we do feel it is important to preserve the author's original work to better understand the attitudes of the audience at the time this book was originally published. Further, we do not feel it is our place to decide what may or may not be appropriate for today's audiences. Individual readers should decide what is best for themselves.

When I left the Royal Huts Inn, on the top of Hind Head, in order to visit the Devil's Punchbowl and Gibbet Hill, immortalized by Turner in the Liber Studiorum, I passed along a wide straight road—the new high road between London and Portsmouth—and shortly came to the edge of the Punchbowl and cast my eyes on its beauty. The fog, which had been heavy in London when I left on this mid-October morning, extended even to Haslemere and hung in the valleys so that the tops of the Surrey hills rose like islands from the sea of mist, and in the brilliant sunshine which glorified these upper levels softened and mellowed all the wide expanse of hill and dale and down which ranged between me and the Southern coast. The hill gave steeply on all sides save the north-west, where the circular valley opened to the plain below. All the summer tints were chastened and mellowed; all the full colours which the sunshine had glorified had faded into the sere of Autumn. The pink and purple of the heather were changed to a brown with only a suggestion of faded colour to warm its tone. The bracken was of rich amber and faded yellow, and the myriads of grasses and wild flowers had donned their winter garb—the hues of decay. Through all this rich mass of Autumn tints, the broom, untouched as yet by the frost, sent an emerald flash. The green bushes which fringed the tiny stream running through the valley seemed of supernatural vividness, and the dark green of the pines which covered the western slope and ran down into the valley seemed to assert in some positive way the right of nature to maintain her own colour despite all influences. Away to the north and west, past the spurs and shoulders of the hill, the woods and valleys, the copses and villages and hills and ridges ranged in endless succession; and it was after a long, long pause that I turned from drinking in the beauty of the scene with my heart full of the power and majesty and purifying influence of nature's beauty. "Here at least," said I to myself, "the soul of man is elevated; and on this higher plane of nature's handiwork the evil of our hearts is lulled."

As I turned, however, I started, for, as if by the irony of fate, there, beside me, was a grim memorial of man's wickedness and lust for blood— a tombstone by the roadside, marking the spot where a century ago a poor seaman trudging on his way from Portsmouth was murdered.

But not the stone only was of interest; for by it were three figures which would have arrested attention anywhere. They were only children, but of types that were not common. Two were young Indian girls of an age which by the slower development of English girlhood would be about some thirteen or fourteen years; being, however, of Eastern birth, they were probably much younger. They stood one on each side of the memorial stone, looking almost like heraldic supporters, as each with a slim brown hand resting on an elbow of the stone, leaned her face on the hand while looking at me gravely with long, dark, fathomless eyes. They were both very pretty of their type, and their slim girlish figures were draped in black of some shimmering material, made in a half Eastern fashion with a wide belt of the stuff round the waist, and some kind of dark material wound around the head and acting as a head gear. The third of the group was a little boy of some ten years old, with hair of spun gold, eyes like blue porcelain, and a winning smile on his rosy face. One might designate him indifferently a Cupid or an angel. He was dressed in a dark blood-coloured tunic.

For a few seconds I stood looking at this group, they regarding me steadfastly without the slightest movement. Then I spoke to them, making some remarks about the beauty of the scene. One of the girls said, tapping the stone with her hand as she spoke.

"Can you tell us anything about this stone, Sir? We are strangers."

"I am a stranger here myself, but I think we will find it here," I answered, as I proceeded to read the inscription, which is on both sides of the stone. When I read the word 'murder,' they all three looked at each other and then at me, and shuddered. Strange to say, they followed the shudder with a smile, though they might be frightened, and I hastened to add—"But you need not let this disturb you. It all happened a hundred years ago, when the country was very different from what it is now." One of the girls said in a low voice, whose tones were peculiarly penetrating,

"I hope not—I trust not;" and the little boy looked up at me with a laugh and said,

"I suppose if there were a murder now, some one would be stuck up on Gibbet Hill!"

"Hallo! young man," said I, "You know all about it, I see. I am going up to the hilltop to see the Memorial Cross. Will you come and see where they put the murderer?"

"With pleasure," he said, with an air of almost supernatural gravity, lifting his cap in acknowledgment of my invitation. The girls bowed too, and we all moved up the hill together. As we went, I noticed that the boy had one of his hands tightly clenched. "What have you got there?" I asked him.

"These!" he said, opening his hand and showing me a crumpled mass of great earthworms, wriggling in their sudden freedom. "I love worms," he went on. "See how they wriggle so, and you can pull them out long!" and he illustrated the latter fact.

"Poor worms!" said I. "Why not let them go? They would much rather be on the ground."

"Shan't," was his only reply, as he shove them into the folds of his tunic.

There were a lot of persons at the cross when we reached the top of Gibbet Hill, besides abundant evidence of recent visitors in the shape of egg-shells and pieces of newspaper—for the cross is a favorite picnicking spot. Amongst the strangers, my fancy was chiefly taken by a lady and gentleman whom I dubbed "the honeymoon couple." I soon became so absorbed by the lovely view that lay stretched before me—a wilderness of rising hilltops with green woods and rich valleys—that I quite forgot my young companions. I went to the edge of the steep hill and sat down looking eastwards, and lost myself in the beauty of the scene.

Presently, I remembered my young companions and looked around for them; but they had quite disappeared—there was not a sight of them anywhere around.

My departure from London had been early, and the walk from Hazlemere in the blazing October sun a little fatiguing, so after a while, when I had been all around the summit of the Head and had, so to speak, boxed the scenic compass, I took my way to a deep shady grove of hazel and beech with tall pines rising over all—one of those dense copses that creep up from the valley, throwing jagged spikes of greenery up the slopes of the hill. Here there was the very perfection of autumn fullness. The undergrowth grew luxuriantly under the shelter of the clustering pines. The brown of the bark and the bluish bloom of the foliage of the pines, as one gazed into the half-dim aisles between them—the sweet aromatic odor which they exhaled—the sleepy silence, accentuated only by the hum of nature's myriad vitalities—the soft, rich grass, whose summer greenery stood untouched as yet in this sheltered dell—all invited repose. With a blissful feeling of content, I stretched myself on the grass and soon lost my thoughts and my consciousness in the interlaced branches above me.

How long I slept, I know not; but it must have been a good while, for I felt thoroughly refreshed as to brain, and with that half-aching sense of cramped muscles which comes after a long period of unchanged attitude; and there was over me that mysterious sense of elapsed time which tells philosophers that our thought is continuous in some form or another. There was, however, no sense of duty omitted—no pressure of coming work, which in such cases destroys the charm of awakening. I knew that there was ample time before freedom, and enjoy the freshness and purity of the air in this wonderful spot.

And so I did not stir, but lay on my back with my hands under my head looking up into the branches and watching the gleams of light struggle through the tracery of leaf and branch. I thought of many things, in that luxurious half-dreamy way which belongs to the leisure of an habitually busy man. Taking up a thread of thought and dropping it again—swaying between general and particular ideas—in all ways realizing that greatest of pleasures, intellectual *laissez aller.*

There was in the air the same faint hum of varied sounds which had at the first lulled me to sleep; but somehow the volume was richer than before—more full and satisfying to the ear, and with a special significance, as if not only all nature was speaking but that there was some one voice amongst the myriad more potent than the rest. I listened with a growing interest, and the sound seemed to take a more definite place amongst nature's harmonies. It was not as if it grew in loudness, but merely as if the vibrations accumulated, coming in waves more quickly than they could die away.

Gradually all the other noises seemed to die away, and I heard only this one sound. It seemed to be closer and closer as I began to distinguish more clearly, until I shortly came to the conclusion that its source was separated from me by only some score of yards. Then I began to be able to analyse it a little. In general effect it was like a sort of musical muffled corncrake—a corncrake in a whisper—but with some subtle prevailing sweetness which seemed of almost irresistible attraction. Presently I raised my head from amongst the bracken where I lay, and looked whence the sound proceeded.

There, to my surprise, in an open dell where the light fell through a break in the trees were grouped the children whom I had seen. The two girls were seated, and between them the little boy stood up. One of the girls held in her left hand something which looked like a set of pandean pipes made of thin canes but slightly thicker than wheaten straws. Across this she drew something attached to the fingers of the right hand, which made the bass of the strange corncrake sound. The other girl held a shell with strings across it which she touched lightly; and the boy had a sort of reed flute which gave forth a peculiarly long sweet note, but which blended in the mass of music. Then the girls joined in a sort of monotonous chant of strange sweetness but very, very faint. They were all three looking well to one side of me. By and by the girls stood up; they all turned slightly, and I could see that they were evidently turning slowly in a complete circle, as though seeking in every direction around them. As they began to face my direction I sank down again into the bracken so that they might not see me, for the affair began to absorb my interest. I took care, however, to peep through the fronds of the bracken and see all that went on. A very short time elapsed before my attention was diverted, and in not the most pleasant of ways.

Hearing a stir and rustle among the dead leaves beside me I looked round, and almost jumped to my feet, for there close by, and approaching closer, was a large snake of the blind-worm species. It came straight towards me and actually passed over my feet. I did not stir, and it went on, heeding me no more than if I had been a log of wood, and wriggled away towards the group in the sunlit glade. It was evidently attracted by the strange, weird music, and as this was my first actual experience of serpent-charming my interest grew, and I watched the little party more closely than before. They went on with their music, and the snake approached closer and closer; till at the feet of the fair-haired child it stopped, and, curling itself into a spiral, raised its head and began to hiss. The boy looked down, and the girls turned their eyes towards him, but the music did not stop for a moment; on the contrary, it grew something quicker. Then the snake twined itself around the child's ankle and began to climb its way up his body, wriggling round and round his leg and thigh, and up and up, till at last it crawled along the arm that held the flute.

Then, suddenly, the music stopped. The two girls stood up, and the boy stretched out his arm with the snake wound around it, with his hand stretched out wide open, the palm upward. The snake remained perfectly still, as if transformed into stone. Then the girls took hands and circled slowly around the boy, uttering a low, whispering, mysterious chant, something the same as the earlier one, but this time in decrescendo as compared with the former crescendo, and in a minor key. This went on for quite two or three minutes. The boy remained perfectly still, with his arm extended, and his blue eyes fixed on the snake. Then the latter raised its head slightly and seemed to follow with it the movements of the circling girls. They continued their slow movement, round and round, the snake's movements being more and more pronounced with each revolution, till presently it was boldly turning, like the automatic motion of a firework, around the boy’s arm. Gradually the motion of the girls got slower and the snake correspondingly less, till, presently, the girls’ movement, and the low droning music, which had never stopped, died away altogether, and the snake hung, a dead mass as limp as a piece of string, across the boy's hand. The boy never moved, but the girls let go each other's hands, and one of them, who had stopped just in front of the boy, took the snake by head and tail and seemed to gently pull it out straight. When she let it go, it lay across the boy's hand as stiff as a piece of wood. There was something uncanny about this which recalled to me recollections of a man whom I had once seen in a cataleptic fit, and whose body retained any position into which it was put, no matter how grotesque or how uncomfortable or strained. The snake seemed to be under some similar condition, and with strange curiosity I awaited the next development. The boy continued impassive, his hand still stretched out and the snake resting across it. The girls stood a little in front of him, one on either side, so that the outstretched hand was midway between them.

Then began some questioning between them in a language which I presumed to be some form of Indian, but which I did not understand. Both voices were sweet, with a peculiar penetrating power, but one of them I seemed instinctively to fear, although it was the sweeter and softer of the two. Somehow—and the idea was quite spontaneous— it seemed to suggest murder. From the tones and inflections of the voices, I gathered that all utterances were put in the form of questions—a supposition shortly confirmed in a strange way, for the answers were given by the rigid snake. When each girl in turn had had her say—and they suggested positive and negative in their tones—the snake would slowly turn around like the needle in a compass, and point its head to either one. The sweeter voice seemed to be the positive, and the other the negative in the inquiry; and in all the earlier questions, the snake, after turning slowly around, remained with its head towards the negative. This first seemed to disturb and then annoy the positive inquirer, and her voice grew more deadly sweet and penetrating until it made me shudder. Then she seemed to get more and more enraged, for her eyes gleamed with a dark unholy light, and at the same time came her question in a keen thrilling whisper. For answer, the snake then spun around quicker and quicker, and suddenly came to a dead stop in front of the other girl.

The disappointed one gave one fierce, short, inhospitable hiss, while a look of deadly malice swept over her face; and then passed away, leaving it as serene as before. At the same instant, the rigidity of the snake collapsed, and it hung for an instant as limp as before, and then slipped to the ground and lay there all in a heap without motion, as if dead. The boy started, as though from sleep to waking, and began to laugh. The girls joined in the cachinnation, and in an instant the glade, which had seemed so weird, grew instinct with laughter, as the children chased each other into the recesses of the wood, and disappeared from view.

Then I rose up from the bracken where I lay. I could hardly believe my eyes, and thought that I must have been sleeping, and have dreamt it all. But there lay the seemingly dead snake before me as a palpable evidence that I had beheld a reality.

The sun was far in the west when I had finished my stroll through the laneways and copses upon the Witley side of Hind Head and found myself once more at its highest point on Gibbet Hill.

The place was now deserted. The picnicers had all gone home; the pony traps and donkeys and parties of school children had disappeared, and nothing remained of the day's visitation but the usual increase in old newspapers and broken egg shells. As the light was just beginning to fade and the air to grow a shade colder, the sense of loneliness was more than ever marked. But I had come from the midst of the hum and turmoil of the city to enjoy this very loneliness, and its luxury was to me unspeakable. Down in the valleys the mist still lay dim and fleecy white, and from it the hill tops rose dark and grim. A belt of cloud fringed the whole horizon, and above it stretched a sea of sulphur yellow, flecked here and there with little clouds of white which, swimming high above the level of the hill, caught the last splendours of the sun, now obscured by the horizon. One or two stars began to twinkle through the darkening sky, and a stillness that seemed sentient stole up through the valley and reached to where I sat.

Then the air grew colder, and the silence became perfect. The stars swam out into the sky, which had now a darker blue, and a soft light fell on the scene. I sat on and on, and drank in the wondrous beauty in which I was immersed. Weariness of mind and body seemed of the dim past, and as if they could never again be other than a sad memory. In such moments a man seems almost to be born again, and to have every faculty renewed to the full. I leaned with my back against the great stone cross, and, putting my hands behind me, clasped my arms around its back so as to change my position and be able to enjoy more fully the luxury of rest.

Suddenly, without a word of warning, each hand was grasped from behind and held tight in a pair of hands, thin and warm but so strong that I could make no movement; and at the same time a scarf or shawl of some light, fleecy, but thick material was thrown over my face and drawn tightly from behind, holding my head close to the stone. So pinioned and gagged, I could neither move nor speak, and had perforce to await the coming events. Then my hands were tied with a string put around the wrists and drawn tight, so that I was fixed more firmly than before. I could hear no sound, and took it for granted that I was being prepared for robbery. I was alone, far away from everyone and in the hands of men stronger than myself, and so resigned myself to the situation as well as I could—secretly thankful that I had only a small sum of money with me. After a time which seemed long, but which was probably of but a few minutes' duration, the scarf was pulled down so far that my eyes were free, though my mouth was still covered and I was unable to cry out.

For a few moments I was too much surprised even to think as strange what I saw before me. Instead of burly footpads with rude manner and coarse force, there were the three children who had arrested my attention earlier in the day. They stood before me perfectly still and silent for a little while, their eyes being the only features which expressed either consciousness or interest of any kind. Two of them, the boy and one girl, then smiled on me with an amused superiority, whilst the other—she who in the glade had exhibited such anger—smiled with a deadly cold hate which, bound as I was, made me shudder. This latter then approached me closer, the others remaining quite still and looking on with their superior amused smile. She took from her waist, where it was concealed in the folds of her dress, a long sharp dagger, thin, double-edged, and lethal-looking. This she proceeded to flourish before me with extraordinary dexterity and rapidity. Half the time its keen edge actually touched my skin, and the contact made me wince. Anon she would dart towards my eyes till I could feel its cold point actually touching my eyeballs. Then she would, as if hurling herself at me with the point of the deadly weapon, directed to my heart, but would stop just as it seemed that my last moment had come. This went on for a little while; but short though it was, it seemed endless. I felt a cold chill, strange numbness, growing over me; my heart seemed to get cold and weak—colder, and colder— weaker and weaker still, till at length my eyes closed. I tried to open them—succeeded; tried again—failed, succeeded—failed—and at length consciousness passed away from me.

The last thing I remember seeing with my waking eyes was the gleam of the long knife in the starlight as it moved in the young girl's dexterous play. The last sound I heard was a low laugh from all three of the children.

The voice in my ears was dim and distant; but it gradually grew louder, and the spoken words became intelligible:—

“Wake up! Wake up, man! You will get your death of cold!”

Cold! The word struck home, for there was at my heart a numbness, and a chill as of death. My consciousness struggled back into existence, and I opened my eyes.

It was now much brighter, for a great yellow moon had arisen, and the common was flooded with its light. Beside me were two persons whom at once I recognized as the “honeymoon couple” of earlier in the day. The man was bending over me and was shaking me roughly by the shoulder, whilst the lady stood by, looking on anxiously, with her hands clasped.

“Is he not dead, George, is he?” I heard her say. The answer came.

“No! thank goodness!—He must have fallen asleep. It is a mercy that you had the inspiration to come out to see the moonlight view from here; he might have died of cold. See! the ground is white with the hoar-frost already. Wake up, man!—Wake up, and come away!”

“My heart,” I murmured, “My heart!” for it was icy cold. The man looked more serious, and said to his wife:—

“Bella, this may be serious. Could you run back to the hotel, and send someone if necessary? It may be that his heart is affected.”

“Certainly, dear; shall I go at once?”

“Wait a minute first.” He leaned over me again. The past was coming back to me quickly, and I asked him:

“Did you see anywhere some children, two Indian girls, and a fair-haired boy?”

“Yes! hours and hours ago, as they went down the London road on a tricycle. They were laughing, and we thought them the prettiest and happiest children we had ever seen. But why?”

"My heart! my heart!" I cried out again, for there was a coldness which seemed to numb me.

The man put his hand over my heart, but quickly tore it away again with a cry of terror.

"What is it, George? What is it?" almost shrieked the lady, for his action was so sudden and unexpected that it thoroughly frightened me.

He stood back, and she clung frightened to his arm, as a large blindworm wriggled itself out from my bosom—fell on the ground—and glided away down the hillside into the copse below.

Printed in Great Britain
by Amazon

51576859R00015